KATIE'S
WORLD

KATIE GOES TO NEW YORK

Karen Mezek

HARVEST HOUSE PUBLISHERS
Eugene, Oregon 97402

MRS. JULIA THOMPSEN

MR. JOHN McABE THOMPSEN

KATIE THOMPSEN

BETH McKINNEY

CANADA

PACIFIC
OCEAN

UNITED STATES

ATLANTIC
OCEAN

CENTRAL
AMERICA

SOUTH
AMERICA

FLAG OF
THE UNITED STATES

PETER THOMPSEN

MRS. AIMEE HOFFMAN

LEAH HOFFMAN

WALTER HERMAN

KATIE GOES TO NEW YORK

Copyright © 1991 by Karen Mezek
Published by Harvest House Publishers
Eugene, Oregon 97402

Library of Congress Cataloging-in-Publication Data

Mezek, Karen, 1956-
   Katie goes to New York / Karen Mezek.
   Summary: As a reward for rescuing a famous opera singer, Katie receives a free trip to
New York City where she uncovers the mystery of how to make one's dreams come true.
   ISBN 0-89081-864-9
   [1. Mystery and detective stories.   2. New York (N.Y.)—
Description—Fiction.]   I. Title.
PZ7.M5748Kas   1991
[Fic]—dc20   90-20594
                                                                                                    CIP
                                                                                                    AC

Printed in the United States of America.

Chapter 1

A Stormy Night

"Hey, batter, batter!"

"Hey, batter!"

Katie tried to ignore the jeers of the other team as she picked up the bat and took a few practice swings. Looking at the pitcher, her eyes narrowed. Tyler Robertson stared back, lips curled in a wicked grin.

"You can't psyche me out, you big bully," Katie said under her breath. "You think you're so great—just wait!"

Tyler wound up and threw the ball. It whizzed right past Katie as she swung wildly.

"Stee-rike!" yelled the umpire.

Tyler's grin became a big smile, revealing his chipped front tooth. Katie tried to stay cool.

Whoosh! She resisted the urge to swing as the ball flew past her.

"Ball one!" cried the umpire.

"Ball two!" came the third call.

Tyler stopped smiling. "This is going to be it," thought Katie. "This will be the one."

Once again, the ball came flying toward her. Katie swung. "Yes!!" she cried, as she watched the white blur quickly become a tiny speck, far beyond the farthest outfielder. It was an easy run around the diamond and Katie paused to stick her tongue out at Tyler before sailing into home base.

Everyone crowded around to congratulate the winning team and their new baseball hero.

"What a hit!"

"You're the best batter in the league!"

"Totally amazing!"

Katie drank it all in. "When I saw Tyler's smug mug, I knew I had to save the day," she said. "I just held that bat steady and—Oh, no, run for cover! It's raining cats and dogs!"

Dark, gray thunderheads, that had been threatening rain all afternoon gave a loud rumble and let loose their heavy load.

Tyler sped past Katie, stomping hard in a puddle. Mud splattered all over her legs and arms. "I'll get you next time, skinny dip," he yelled.

"What a creep," said Beth, Katie's best friend. Together they ran across the green field and up the hill to Katie's house.

Katie's mom, Mrs. Julia Thompsen, was waiting inside. "What a downpour! Thank goodness it didn't spoil the game. You were stupendous, Katie!" She gave her daughter a big hug. "I'm just sorry your father is away and couldn't see your home run."

Katie's father, Mr. John McAbe Thompsen, was a foreign correspondent and spent much of his time traveling to exciting parts of the world. He'd even taken Katie and her brother Peter and Beth along on a couple of adventures.

After changing out of their wet clothes, Katie

and Beth headed for the kitchen. Mrs. Thompsen had homemade chicken noodle soup and thick slices of warm bread and butter waiting for them. It wasn't long before Katie's brother, Peter, joined them.

"Pretty good batting," he told her.

"Everybody groans when I come up to bat," Beth said. "But Katie's the best. She's a star!"

Katie almost choked on her soup. "A star! Yeah, right! I wish I was a movie star, or something like that. But a baseball star in the small town of Cambria, California? Forget it!"

Mrs. Thompsen laughed. "You don't know what you're saying. I'm sure that being a big star isn't as wonderful as it seems."

A loud clap of thunder and a bolt of lightning made everyone jump.

Peter ran to the window and looked out. "It's really coming down. There's a river in the middle of the driveway!"

Although it was still summer, and early evening, the sky was dark. Beth called her parents and asked if she could spend the night at Katie's. When that was taken care of, they all settled down to a cozy game of Monopoly.

By nine o'clock, the two girls were yawning and rubbing their tired eyes. Mrs. Thompsen prayed earnestly for Katie's father, who was far away in London attending an important conference. Then she kissed the children good-night. Carrying steaming mugs of hot chocolate, Katie and Beth headed down the hallway for bed. Rain pounded against the windows and flashes of lightning made jagged shadows dance about the room.

Suddenly both girls stopped and listened. "Do you hear what I hear?" asked Katie.

"Someone's knocking at the door," said Beth.

Then they heard another sound. A muffled voice called, "Help! Help me!"

Quickly they ran to the front door.

"Who is it?" cried Katie. No one answered.

"Who's out there?" she called again. Still no response.

By this time Katie's mother had joined them. When the faint voice again cried, "Please, let me in," she undid the latch and slowly started to open the door. Something was leaning hard on the other side, and the door flung open before anyone could stop it. Wind and rain rushed in as a dark shape fell motionless at their feet.

Katie and Beth screamed. All they could see was a heavy coat and a mass of wet hair streaming across the tiles. Gingerly, Mrs. Thompsen turned the figure over. The dim hall light revealed the face of a beautiful black woman with a long jagged cut on her forehead.

Moaning softly, the woman turned her head from side to side. "Let's see if we can get her onto the sofa," said Katie's mom. With all three helping, they managed to get her to her feet. Leaning heavily on Mrs. Thompsen, the injured woman staggered to the living room and collapsed on the sofa.

"Thank you," she said in a feeble voice. "My car . . . a terrible accident." Her head drooped and her eyes closed.

"What's going on in here?" came Peter's voice.

He switched the lights on and the bright glare lit up the woman's face.

Katie gasped . . . Beth gasped . . . Mrs. Thompsen gasped. All three looked more closely at the sleeping figure.

"I can't believe it," said Mrs. Thompsen in awe. "It's . . . it's Aimee Hoffman—*the* Aimee Hoffman."

"I think I'm going to faint," whispered Katie.

Peter shook his head in disbelief and said, "I must be dreaming. I'm going back to bed!"

Chapter 2

Stage Struck

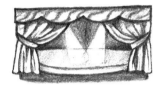

Mrs. Thompsen called Dr. Fischer, who lived down the street, and he hurried over to offer his help.

"Suffering from shock and a slight concussion, I'd say. Best thing would be a good night's sleep. I'll look in on her again in the morning." He stared down at the woman curiously. "Sure would like to know what she's doing in our neck of the woods. Imagine, Aimee Hoffman—the opera star!"

Mrs. Thompsen made sure their unexpected guest was settled comfortably. "Now, it's off to bed for the rest of us," she said. "What a night!"

The next morning dawned bright and clear. Katie and Beth hopped out of bed early and hurried down the hall. It was hard to believe the most famous opera singer in the world was asleep in the living room! Cautiously they peeked around the corner.

"She's not awake yet," whispered Katie. "Let's go in the kitchen and make some coffee, so when she wakes up it'll be ready. Mom's still asleep too."

Beth made fresh squeezed orange juice while Katie did the coffee and toast.

"We can put it on a tray and bring it to her," Katie suggested.

They found their guest sitting up, carefully feeling the bandage on her head. Seeing the two girls, she smiled.

"You saved my life," she told them. "How can I ever thank you?"

"Oh, we didn't really *do* anything," Katie said shyly.

"Actually," added Beth, "you kind of fell into the house and we dragged you over to the sofa. Wow, were we scared!"

"Are you feeling any better?" Katie asked.

"Oh, yes! Just the smell of that coffee has done wonders for me already!"

Katie and Beth watched as two graceful, slender hands, tipped by perfectly shaped pale pink nails reached for the coffee mug. Her lips took a delicate sip and let out a long, satisfied sigh. Large dark eyes looked at the two girls. "And now," she said, "I don't think I know the names of my rescuers."

"Oh!" said Katie, feeling the color rise on her cheeks. "I'm Katie Thompsen."

"I'm Beth McKinney. I live down the street."

The woman gave them a dazzling smile. "And I am Aimee Hoffman."

A tiny scream from the hallway made everyone turn and stare. There was Mrs. Thompsen, her eyes wide and her hand clapped over her mouth. "So it is you," she said in a rush. "I could scarcely believe it last night, but now I can see it's true! Oh, Mrs. Hoffman, I'm your biggest fan!"

11

Katie looked at her mother in astonishment. Never in all her life had she seen her so flustered!

At that moment a still sleepy Peter appeared and stomped his foot impatiently, "Would somebody please tell me what's going on around here?"

Aimee Hoffman laughed deeply. "Now, there's a boy who does *not* know who I am! Fortunately, being an opera singer doesn't always mean people recognize me, although I'm flattered that you three did."

A knock on the door announced the return of Dr. Fischer. He had brought Mrs. Hoffman's suitcase with him from her car. "You must have skidded in the rain around that dangerous turn. Quite a nasty accident!"

Mrs. Hoffman shivered. "My husband died in a car crash years ago. Thank God I was spared this time!" She was sad for a few moments, but it wasn't long before her smile returned.

After examining his patient, Dr. Fischer congratulated her on her quick recovery. Then he left, clutching a piece of paper with Mrs. Hoffman's autograph scrawled across it.

While their visitor took a shower and changed her clothes, Katie and Beth ate bowls of cereal at the kitchen table. Pointing with her spoon, Katie said,

"Now, what do you suppose a big star like that is doing in a place like this?"

Beth shrugged her shoulders. "What most people do. She's come here for a vacation—to get away from New York and all those horrible fans!"

Katie shook her head. "*The* Aimee Hoffman doesn't take a vacation in Cambria, no way! She'd go to France, or Tahiti, or someplace wonderful."

"Well, whatever her reason, it's none of our business," Beth warned her friend. She knew that when Katie became curious about something, she didn't rest until she found out every detail. More than once Katie's curiosity had gotten her into trouble, and Beth tried her hardest to protect her best friend from her wild imagination.

13

"Oh, come on!" replied Katie. "I haven't written in my diary for days because everything's been so boring. But after last night, I'll be able to write pages and pages!" She leaned forward, her brown eyes sparkling, "And who knows what other juicy bits of information I'll be able to find out!"

Beth rolled her eyes in despair. "Katie Thompsen, you're hopeless! Will you ever learn to keep your nose out of other people's affairs?"

"Nope!" came the hearty answer.

When Mrs. Hoffman returned, looking elegant and refreshed, Katie blurted out, "How did you end up way out here, in the middle of a dark, stormy night?"

There was a long pause, and Beth was sure the famous star was going to tell Katie to mind her own business. But instead she smiled her beautiful smile and said, as if she hadn't heard a word, "Such a lovely day! Shall we go for a walk?"

Katie led the way up the hill behind her house to the old oak tree. "This is my secret place. Nobody ever comes here except me and Beth." She climbed up the trunk and reached her hand into a crevice between the branches. "My hidden treasure," she said, holding out an old tin box for Mrs. Hoffman to see.

The singer's dark eyes sparkled. "What's inside? Diamonds and rubies?"

Katie laughed. "I wish! No, it's only my diary!"

"She writes all her adventures in it. And believe me, she's had quite a few! Actually, we both have," Beth said proudly.

Mrs. Hoffman looked impressed. "It sounds like that diary is worth much more than diamonds or rubies. Inside are all your hopes and dreams."

"I want to be a writer when I grow up, just like my dad," Katie explained. She put the tin box back and climbed down again. "Only sometimes I get discouraged. Hopes and dreams aren't good enough if they're just make-believe. How do you actually make them happen?"

Katie and Beth waited expectantly for the answer. Aimee Hoffman seemed so successful and self-assured. If anyone could tell them how to make their dreams come true, she could.

"Ah, that's a good question," the singer said softly. Shading her eyes from the sun, she looked down the hill toward the ocean. She seemed very far away for a moment.

"I suppose I could give you an answer to that question, but I think it would be better for you to discover it for yourselves." She put an arm around each of them and headed back to the house. "And I have a wonderful idea of how to make that happen!"

Try as they might, the two girls could not get any more information out of Mrs. Hoffman. When the singer told them she would have to leave the next day for New York, Katie felt sad and deflated. She hadn't found out anything about the famous star! She hadn't even discovered what Aimee Hoffman had been doing in their small sea-side town on such a stormy night.

Chapter 3

An Invitation

Katie and Beth sat perched on a rock over-looking the ocean. Huge waves crashed beneath them and seagulls soared overhead. Both girls stared at the water.

"What'll we do today?" asked Katie glumly.

Beth shrugged her shoulders. "Dunno."

A whole week had passed since Mrs. Hoffman's strange arrival. She had come and gone so suddenly, it was hard to believe she had ever been there at all. Without her, the days seemed long and empty.

"Katie, Beth!" came a voice from behind them. Katie looked up to see her mother walking down the hill.

"I've brought you some lunch," she said, stepping onto the rock beside them and handing out paper bags. "I also brought you a letter," she added with a big smile.

Katie eagerly grabbed the white envelope. When she saw the return address, she squealed and tore it open. Together, the two girls read the pages.

"I knew it!" cried Katie. "I knew she wouldn't forget us!"

Both girls looked as if they were about to burst with excitement. "You'll never believe what she says!" exclaimed Beth, handing Mrs. Thompsen the letter.

Mrs. Thompsen's eyes grew round and a hand went to her heart as if to slow it down. "This is very generous of Mrs. Hoffman. Certainly, I expected a thank you note—but free airline tickets and an invitation to the Metropolitan Opera House in New York? I can't believe it!"

"Well, can we go?" Katie asked anxiously.

"I'll have to see if I can reach your father. If he gives the okay, then so do I!"

"Hurray!" cried the two girls.

Scrambling to their feet, they raced up the hill. "Let's ask my parents right now!" cried Beth.

Katie and Beth found the McKinneys gardening in the backyard. Jumping up and down like yo-yos, the two girls explained what had happened

Then they collapsed on their knees and pleaded with all their might. With a personal invitation from the star herself and free airline tickets, Beth's parents couldn't possibly refuse.

Back to Katie's house they flew, to find Mrs. Thompsen on the telephone with Katie's father. When she hung up her face was beaming.

"New York City, here we come!" she cried.

"Not me," Peter said, angrily throwing his baseball cap on the kitchen table. "No way do I want to travel across the country just to listen to a bunch of weirdos make high-pitched squeals all night long! I'd rather stay here with Jeff!"

"And so you shall," Mrs. Thompsen assured him. "I have no desire to torture you, Peter, so don't worry!"

"Phew!" he said with relief. "Wait 'til I tell Jeff. We'll have a great time!" Off he ran, slamming the front door behind him.

"Actually, I'm not so crazy about opera, either," Beth confessed later as they were packing Katie's suitcase. "The singing sounds kind of funny and you can't understand a word they're saying. I mean, it doesn't have a beat or anything!"

Katie stuck her nose in the air and said in a superior voice, "Beth McKinney, don't show your ignorance. You obviously have no culture!"

"Well, excuuuuse me," Beth retorted, giving her friend a good push.

"Oops..." she cried, as she watched Katie fall across the suitcase and then onto the floor, followed by all her neatly folded clothes.

"That's the last time I ever ask you to help me pack," said Katie, laughing good-naturedly.

The next morning found Mrs. Thompsen, Katie and Beth aboard flight 106, bound for New York.

"Just think," said Katie when the plane was airborne, "we've had all kinds of adventures in other countries, but we haven't really seen anything of the United States."

"I'm glad you'll have an opportunity to do that now," answered Mrs. Thompsen. "God has blessed our country with so much, and it's important to appreciate that. Also, it's our duty to learn about our homeland so we can help it to grow even better."

When they arrived at La Guardia airport in New York, it was early evening. Mrs. Thompsen was about to flag down a taxi when a gentleman wearing a suit and chauffeur's cap approached them.

"Excuse me, Mrs. Thompsen?" he asked, speaking with a proper British accent.

"Why, yes," said Mrs. Thompsen, surprised.

The man gave a slight bow. "Walter Herman, at your service. I have been instructed by Mrs. Hoffman to meet you. Will you please follow me?"

He led the travelers to a long, sleek limousine and opened the door with a flourish. Dark leather seats and a thick carpet greeted them inside. Beneath the special glass barrier that separated them from the driver was a teak wood cabinet filled with soft drinks and bottled water, to be served in crystal glasses. The windows were tinted so no one could see in.

"Welcome to New York," said the chauffeur, sliding back the glass window. "Mrs. Hoffman has instructed me to take you to the Hotel Pierre, with her compliments."

"The Hotel Pierre!" said Mrs. Thompsen. She whispered to Katie and Beth worriedly, "It's so very expensive!"

"Is there some way I can reach Mrs. Hoffman to speak with her?" she asked out loud.

"Mrs. Hoffman has a very busy schedule, but I'm sure she will be contacting you later this evening."

Katie's mother shook her head in disbelief. "I never imagined she would go to so much trouble. It makes me feel uncomfortable."

"Oh, come on, Mom," said Katie. "This is probably no big deal for such a rich and famous person. Just sit back and have fun!"

Soon, even Mrs. Thompsen had started to
relax as she pointed out the sights to Katie and
Beth. Both girls gasped when, crossing Manhattan
bridge, they saw the sparkling New York skyline.

"If you really want to take your breath away,
we can look at the city from the top of the World
Trade Center. Do you know, it's so big, it has its
own zip code! And it has 110 stories!"

"One hundred and ten stories!" Beth
shrieked. "I think I just developed a fear of
heights!"

Before long, they had arrived at the Hotel
Pierre, where a luxurious suite awaited them.
Vases of fresh flowers filled the room with the
scent of lilies and roses. Beneath one especially
large bouquet was a note written on creamy white
paper edged with gold.

Mrs. Thompsen read the note aloud:

"Welcome to New York! It is my greatest pleasure to have you here. I'm sorry I cannot greet you in person, but I have a very busy schedule today. Tomorrow my chauffeur will pick you up at nine o'clock and bring you to the Opera House. I'll be in rehearsal, but I think you will find it interesting to watch. Then we can have lunch together. I look forward to seeing you!

Yours sincerely,

Aimee Hoffman"

Katie and Beth jumped up and down on their huge double bed. "What a great way to travel!" Katie cried happily.

"Yes," said Mrs. Thompsen, her worried look returning. "We hardly know the woman, and here she is taking such good care of us. Why?" She shook her head in wonder. "I'm calling your father first thing tomorrow morning to tell him all about it. I certainly hope we've done the right thing in coming!"

Chapter 4

Glitter and Gold

Early the next morning, Mrs. Thompsen was on the phone. When she hung up, she looked much happier.

"Thank goodness!" she said. "Your father's responsibilities in London end tomorrow and he'll fly to join us on Saturday. That makes me feel much better!"

"Hurray!" cried Katie.

"That's great!" added Beth. "Your dad is so much fun!"

The telephone buzzed to announce the arrival of Mrs. Hoffman's limousine.

"Good morning, ladies," said the chauffeur, greeting them in the lobby. "As I already mentioned, my name is Walter Herman. But you can call me Wally."

Katie and Beth tried not to giggle. It was hard

to imagine such a proper gentleman being addressed by such an "improper" name.

As they drove down Broadway, Wally began pointing out the sights. He seemed to be enjoying his role as tour guide and was much less formal than he had been the day before.

"The Metropolitan Opera House is called the Met for short. It's a part of The Lincoln Center," he explained, pulling up to the stage door entrance. "There's no place like it in the whole world. Just walking inside on a Saturday evening, with all the chandeliers lit up like diamonds and the women rustling past in their jewels and gowns, is enough to make your scalp tingle and your heart go thump!"

Katie's heart was already going thump, thump. Imagine, backstage at the Met! The door opened and they were led inside by a young woman in jeans and a tee shirt. She hurried them through a dark corridor and down some stairs. Pulling back a heavy curtain, they found themselves in front of the orchestra pit of the vast theater. Quickly the three visitors sat down and looked up at the stage.

"No, no, NO!" cried a familiar voice. "I will *not* come in and walk around this way. It's awkward—it doesn't make sense!"

Standing center stage, eyes flashing, foot tapping, was Mrs. Aimee Hoffman. A faded blue warm-up suit and tennis shoes did nothing to hide her unmistakable star quality.

"She's taller than I remembered," Beth whispered to Katie.

The singer seemed to tower above everyone, especially the little man in front of her with whom she was arguing.

"I come in from *there*," she said, pointing with her long arm. "And I walk straight down. The others on stage will just have to part for me."

The little man thought for a moment and shrugged his shoulders. "You're the boss," he said at last. "Who wants to argue with the boss?"

Everyone on stage held their breath. Fortunately, Mrs. Hoffman's fury melted into a dazzling smile and they all laughed and sighed with relief.

Katie, Beth and Mrs. Thompsen watched spellbound as the rehearsal resumed. The little man seemed to be everywhere at once. He ran around pushing people into place and helping the dancers with a short routine. In the theater chairs, not far from Katie, sat two men and one woman. They were silent most of the time, but when they did talk, everyone stopped and listened carefully, even the star herself.

Shortly before lunch, a man appeared who seemed to be almost as important as Mrs. Hoffman. Tall and slightly stout, he was obviously the other lead in the production.

"He's not handsome enough," Katie objected. But the moment he began to sing, she forgot all about his looks. And when he and Aimee Hoffman sang together, it seemed they were made for each other.

A lunch break was announced at twelve o'clock and Katie was amazed to find the time had passed so quickly.

"I think I'll be an actress when I grow up," Beth announced excitedly. "Or maybe I won't wait 'til I grow up—I'll start right now! I'd be great at it—and it'd be so incredible!"

"Earth to Beth, earth to Beth. Come in, do you read me?" teased Katie. "What happened to my down-to-earth, practical friend? The stage lights must have fried your brain!"

29

"Thanks a lot!" Beth answered. "But you're probably right. I'd die of fright if I had to be up on that stage!"

The three visitors looked around, thinking they'd been forgotten. But suddenly Aimee Hoffman appeared, holding out her arms to give each one a hug.

"How happy I am that you've come!" she cried. "Just let me change, and I'll take you to a wonderful little restaurant!"

The singer disappeared again and they were led back outside by the same young woman who had met them when they arrived.

Wally was waiting by the stage door.

"Did Madame and the two young ladies have an enjoyable morning?" he inquired properly.

"Oh, come on," Katie kidded him. "How can we call you Wally when you act so stuffy?"

Wally's eyes twinkled. "Okay then—how did it go, folks?"

"Great!" cried Katie.

"Fantastic!" echoed Beth.

Mrs. Thompsen smiled. "A wonderful experience. This whole trip is something we'll never forget."

The stage door swung open and Mrs. Hoffman

appeared. "I'm starving!" she said, climbing into the limousine. "Wally, take us to lunch!"

"Yes, Madame," he replied.

As they drove off, the car phone rang. Mrs. Hoffman picked up the receiver. "Hello? . . . Oh, hello, darling! That's wonderful! We'll look forward to seeing you. Goodbye—love you!"

"I have someone very special I would like to introduce you to at lunch," the singer explained.

Katie nudged Beth. A romance—how exciting! And it looked as if they would get to meet the mystery man!

Mrs. Thompsen cleared her throat and began awkwardly, "Mrs. Hoffman—"

"Please call me Aimee," she interrupted.

"Very well . . . Aimee, I just want to thank you for taking such good care of us. Really, it's quite overwhelming! You must be very busy, and to take so much time off for our sake . . . and the hotel . . . well, it's so beautiful. Really, I—"

Aimee laid a hand on Mrs. Thompsen's arm. "I know exactly how you feel, believe me," she reassured her. "But you were so kind to me during a difficult time and I very much wanted to do something for you in return."

Turning to Katie and Beth, she said, "Do you remember the question you asked me under your oak tree?"

The two girls had to think for a moment before answering. "Why, yes," said Katie. "We asked how our dreams could come true."

"Right! And I said I had a wonderful way to show you. Well," she said, throwing out her arms, "this is it! I'm not going to answer your question with words, I'm going to let you discover it for yourselves. Hopefully, by the end of your stay here, you'll have figured it out."

Katie and Beth were puzzled. They hadn't realized their visit was going to include trick questions!

"I'll give you one clue, though," she offered. "Things aren't always what they seem. Or, in other words, all that glitters is not gold!"

Chapter 5

The Mystery Guest

Wally drove down a narrow street in Greenwich Village and pulled up in front of a tiny
Italian restaurant. Cars were jammed in
everywhere and Katie wondered how he would
find a parking place. Then she remembered that
he was their chauffeur and she didn't need to
worry about things like that!

Wally got out and opened the door. Immediately, five horns blared behind them and a
taxi driver stuck his head out of the window,
yelling, "Hey, you big gas guzzler, quit hoggin'
the road!"

"Don't drivers here have any manners?" asked
Katie.

"Of course not," Wally answered. "Everyone
gives everyone else a hard time—it's a New York
tradition!"

Katie and Beth decided they liked Greenwich Village very much. The low buildings and lively streets reminded them of Europe. Everywhere were little cafes with tables spilling out onto the sidewalks. Street musicians, jugglers and acrobats performed in any free space they could find.

Mrs. Hoffman was greeted at the door of the restaurant by the maitre d' and they were quickly ushered in. Walking between the tables, Katie could feel everyone staring and could hear their whispers.

"Do my pants have a rip—is my face dirty?" she whispered to Beth.

"No, silly," Beth whispered back. "Nobody's staring at *you*. They're staring at Mrs. Hoffman!"

Thank goodness! she thought. She wasn't used to making such a grand entrance!

When they had been seated, a large woman with eyes nearly popping out of her head rushed up to their table. She thrust a piece of paper under Aimee's nose and gushed, "Oh, Mrs. Hoffman, *would* you be so kind?" Graciously, the opera singer signed her name.

Holding the paper to her heart, the woman cried, "Thank you! I knew when I woke up this morning something *wonderful* would happen!" Lowering her voice, she confided, "I'm somewhat of an opera singer myself, you know. I could have been great—GREAT! But I had to sacrifice my career... I won't go into the details..." She dabbed at her eyes with a hanky.

Mercifully, the waiter came at that moment

and the woman went away—but not before thanking Mrs. Hoffman for her autograph a great many times!

One chair at their table was empty and Katie and Beth waited impatiently for the mystery guest to arrive.

Suddenly Aimee cried loudly, "Hello! We're over here, darling!"

Katie and Beth looked around eagerly but spotted no dashing suitor. Instead, they saw a teenage girl wave in response. Slowly, she started walking toward them, a long white stick tap-tapping against the chairs and floor. With a shock, Katie realized the girl was blind.

Mrs. Hoffman got up and led her the rest of the way to the table.

"This is my daughter, Leah," she announced, giving her a big hug. "She's a very busy young lady, but fortunately she was able to join us."

Leah smiled a dazzling smile. With smooth chocolate-brown skin and eyes soft as velvet night, she looked just like her mother.

"At last I get to eat," declared Mrs. Hoffman. "If my stomach rumbles one more time, everyone will think it's an earthquake!"

Leah laughed. "You wouldn't believe the amount of pasta my mama can eat, especially when she's rehearsing Italian opera!"

"What is it that keeps you so busy?" Mrs. Thompsen asked Leah with curiosity.

"I study the violin," she explained.

"She does more than that," Mrs. Hoffman added proudly. "Leah has been chosen to compete at the Tchaikovsky Festival in Moscow! And she's only just turned seventeen!"

"Oh, mama, would you be quiet? Do your parents embarrass you as much as my mother does me?" she asked Katie and Beth.

"Well, I guess they would if we did anything half as exciting as you do," said Beth.

"But we don't," added Katie glumly. "We're just boring ol', ordinary kids."

Mrs. Hoffman shook her finger at Katie. "Why don't you and I switch shoes for a day— we'll see how you like it!"

After a wonderful lunch spent slurping up pasta and getting to know their new friends better, the three Californians were ready for some sight-seeing.

"I'd love to join you," said Aimee Hoffman, "but I must get back to my rehearsal. Wally should be here any minute to pick you up. I'll take a taxi. Goodbye!" Before they could protest, she was gone.

"May I join your sight-seeing party?" Leah asked.

"Oh, yes!" Katie and Beth answered enthusiastically.

"Wonderful!" said Mrs. Thompsen. "There are a few shops I would like to visit on my own, so I'll leave you all in the capable hands of Mr. Walter Herman." Wally bowed and doffed his cap.

"I'll see you back at the hotel later," she added, flagging down a taxi.

"All aboard for the sight-seeing adventure of a life-time!" Wally announced.

Chapter 6

Another Clue

Leah and Wally made a funny pair of tour guides, interrupting each other constantly. A contest to see who knew the most about each tourist spot ended with more laughing than talking.

Later in the afternoon, the tour stopped in Central Park. With its shady trees and wide open spaces, it was a great relief after the skyscrapers and narrow streets of the city.

Leah held onto Katie's arm as they walked through the park. The older girl's head tilted up, and a smile was on her lips. Although she could see nothing, she felt the wind upon her face and smelled the flowers and grass around her. No one seemed happier than Leah Hoffman.

"Do you hear that bird singing?" she asked. "It's a skylark. I can tell the names of all the birds in this park by their song—or their squawk! I learned it when I was quite small, to pass the time."

"Can I ask you something?" said Katie. Beth listened nervously. Her friend could come up with the most awkward questions!

"Of course," Leah answered.

"Well, I hope you don't mind, but I was wondering..." Katie took a deep breath. "It must be hard to be blind, knowing everyone around you can see. Do you ever get mad and think it's just not fair?"

Beth groaned, but Leah didn't seem to mind. "Of course I think that—lots of times! But thankfully, God has helped me to deal with those feelings. In one way, I've learned to accept my blindness, by not becoming bitter and letting it destroy me. In another way, I've learned to *not* accept it, by fighting to fulfill my dreams, no matter how great the obstacles."

Fulfilling dreams? Katie and Beth looked at each other. Here was another clue!

Returning to their room later that afternoon, the two girls took off their shoes and collapsed on the bed. Wiggling hot, tired toes, they thought about what Leah had told them.

"Could it be that making dreams come true simply means a lot of hard work and determination?" Beth wondered.

"I think that's part of it," said Katie. "But it can't be everything. Remember our other clue—'all that glitters is not gold.' Somehow, I'm sure Mrs. Hoffman's visit to Cambria could give us the answer. If we could just get her to tell us what she was doing there!"

Beth was exasperated. "Why do you keep talking about that? It's just your wild imagination. Besides, you heard what she said: 'I'm not going to tell you the answer, I'm going to let you find it out for yourselves.'"

"I know, but it sure is driving me crazy!"

Beth yawned loudly. "I'm too tired for anything to drive me crazy." She rolled over and closed her eyes.

Mrs. Thompsen returned to find both girls sprawled across the big bed, fast asleep. Quietly, she placed two brightly wrapped packages on the floor beside them and went to take a shower.

From far away, Katie and Beth heard the telephone ring, then the sound of someone talking. "Yes, that would be wonderful! We'll see you then."

"Wake up, sleepy heads," said the unwelcome voice. "You've been dreaming for almost an hour."

Katie groaned and rolled over.

"Ow," moaned Beth. "You just hit me in the face."

"Uh? Oh, sorry," mumbled Katie.

Beth raised herself up on one elbow and caught sight of the packages. "What's this?" she asked, suddenly wide awake.

44

Katie peeked over her shoulder. "Presents! Mom, did you do that?"

"Open them up, then jump out of bed. We've got plans for the evening."

Eagerly, the girls unwrapped their gifts. Two identical music boxes were revealed, delicately carved and painted. The famous composer Mozart, wearing a powdered wig and embroidered jacket, sat behind a silver grand piano. When the lid of the piano was lifted, the music box played a tune from one of his famous operas, *The Marriage of Figaro.*

"Oh, they're beautiful! Thank you!"

"You're welcome," said Mrs. Thompsen, giving them each a hug. "Now, jump out of bed. Leah's mother has invited us to hear her daughter perform at their church tonight."

Hurriedly, they got ready and raced downstairs to meet Wally once again. Katie was beginning to take the limousine and expensive hotel for granted. If only she were rich and famous, how wonderful it would be!

Climbing into the limousine, Katie felt her discontent growing. Gloomily, she stared out the window.

It wasn't until much later that she began to

wonder where in the world they were going. As
night fell, the streets became dark and desolate.
Unpleasant stories of New York crime and
violence filled Katie's mind. Far in the distance,
the comforting lights and tall buildings of the
central city faded from view.

Even Wally, hunched over the steering wheel
and whistling through his teeth, appeared
frightening to Katie. Perhaps he was really a
member of some gang and was about to murder
them in a dark alley!

A voice broke into Katie's thoughts, startling
her. "Here we are," Wally said, pulling up outside
an old building. Papers littered the street and dark
figures loitered in doorways and under street
lamps. Above the entrance, a pale shaft of light
shined upon the words "THE LORD'S TABER-
NACLE" in large, cracked letters. Katie, Beth and
Mrs. Thompsen got out of the car. Certainly, this
wasn't anything like what they had expected!

Wally and his friends joined the scores of
other people squeezing through the entrance door.
He led them up a side stairway and onto the
balcony. From there they had a fine view of the
platform below. It wasn't long before every seat
in the large church was taken. Katie, Beth and

Mrs. Thompsen looked out on a sea of black, joyful faces. Those seated around them greeted the visitors with a big smile and a loud "Praise the Lord!"

Hot and stuffy, Katie sat perched on an uncomfortable chair. "I wish I were back in my nice hotel room," she thought unhappily. "I could be watching a movie or something."

"Welcome to our festival of music and worship!" cried the bespectacled pastor. Then an enormous choir, all dressed in long white robes, rose from behind him and started to sing.

Katie immediately forgot her discomfort. The words and music poured over the audience,

making Katie want to cry during the slow songs and clap her hands and stomp her feet during the fast ones.

"Mrs. Hoffman's singing, too," Beth said, pointing her out in the choir.

Sure enough, there she was, singing and swaying along with the others.

As a special finale, Leah came forward with her violin. The blind girl placed the instrument under her chin and closed her eyes. Beneath her bow, the strings sang notes of pure joy and aching beauty.

That night Katie lay in her hotel bed staring at the fancy ceiling.

"All that glitters is not gold," she repeated softly. "And maybe some things that don't glitter are better than gold." She smiled to herself and fell asleep.

Chapter 7

The Opera!

The next morning Katie and Beth jumped out of bed excitedly. Katie's father would arrive soon, and tonight they would all go to the opera!

"But what will we wear?" Katie asked her friend, suddenly horrified. "You heard what Wally said about all the ladies in their long dresses and jewels. We don't have anything like that!"

Frantically, the two girls searched through the clothes they had brought.

"Our dresses will never do!" Beth wailed in despair, sinking to the floor.

Katie plopped down next to her. "You're right," she said gloomily.

A sharp knock made Katie bounce up again, saying, "Maybe that's my mom and dad back from the airport."

"Why, Leah!" she exclaimed, opening the door.

49

"Hello," their friend answered, holding out her hand for Katie to lead her inside. Draped over her arm were four dresses.

"I can only stay a minute—Wally's waiting for me downstairs. I brought you some of my clothes. They're way too small for me now and I thought you might have fun trying them on. If you don't want to, just say so and I'll take them back," she finished anxiously.

"Oh, no!" Katie and Beth assured her.

"We'd love to try them on. Oh, they're beautiful!" Beth exclaimed, touching the lovely fabric.

"Good!" Leah said. "If they fit, I'd like you to keep them. Now, I have to go. I'll see you tonight."

Katie and Beth accompanied her to the elevator, thanking her over and over. Then they ran back to the room and inspected the dresses more closely.

"They're *so* beautiful!" said Katie.

"Yeah," said Beth, eyeing the satin dress Katie was trying on. "I just hope we don't fight over them!"

In the end, both were able to choose the two dresses they liked without arguing. And fortunately, they all fit perfectly. The difficult question was which ones they should wear that night.

"I think you should wear the green velvet because it goes with your dark hair," Beth said, batting her eyelashes.

"And you should wear the pale pink because it matches your peaches and cream complexion." Katie pinched her friend's rosy cheeks.

"Stop that!" Beth laughed.

When Mrs. Thompsen and Katie's father arrived back from the airport, they found the two girls all dressed up and parading in front of the mirror. Katie ran to give her dad a hug and enthusiastically told all about Leah's gift.

"Mrs. Hoffman and her daughter certainly have been kind," said Mr. Thompsen. "I look forward to meeting them. But since that won't happen until tonight, what do you say we take a trip to the World Trade Center and go up to the top? I hear Beth loves tall buildings!"

"Yikes," Beth moaned. "Do you mean I'll have to ride the elevator up all those stories and then look down? I can't believe I said your dad was fun, Katie."

"I am fun," he cried. "That's why I'm going to take you up that elevator!"

51

Much to her surprise, Beth survived the ride all the way to the 110th floor. Once there, Katie had to drag her to the edge to look down on the city.

"Help!" Beth gasped when she saw how high they were. "What are those wispy things down there?"

"Clouds, silly," Katie told her.

"I'm going to die, I'm really going to die!" Beth screeched.

When it came time to go down, Beth couldn't decide which was worse—to stay up on top or get back in the elevator. Finally, they convinced her there was no other way to get to the ground again.

"Unless you jump," Katie teased.

"Just think of tonight and that gorgeous dress you get to wear," Mrs. Thompsen encouraged her.

Beth took a deep breath. "Okay, let's go." She stepped into the elevator and kept her eyes closed all the way down.

"I made it. I'm still alive!" she cried, jumping out. "Get me away from this place. I never want to see another skyscraper!"

Katie and Beth could hardly wait for the evening to arrive. They kept asking Katie's parents if it was time to get ready and the answer was always an exasperated *no!* But at last the moment came when they were able to put on their dresses and fix their hair.

"This is a disaster!" Katie cried, staring in the mirror in frustration. She was desperately trying to curl her hair with a curling iron, but it was so straight the curl wouldn't hold.

"How about mine?" Beth wailed. She'd put gobs of sculpting gel on her curly locks to make them calm down, but instead they stuck out in every direction.

Mrs. Thompsen came to the rescue. Curling, spraying, poofing and patting, she transformed their wild hairdos into works of art. Katie and Beth sighed with relief when she was finished.

"Thank goodness," said Katie. "Now we don't look like a couple of clowns."

At the stroke of seven, Wally arrived to take them to the opera. They pulled up in front of the Met along with all the other fancy cars.

Katie stepped out into the warm evening air. "I'm tingling all over."

"Me, too," Beth added. "And I have goose bumps."

"That's what Broadway does to you," Wally said. "The opera, the theater, the ballet—it all makes you tingle from head to toe."

Katie stood still, breathing in the excitement around her. "I have to make sure I remember every detail so I can write it all in my diary," she told Beth. Then she fluffed up her dress and followed her parents inside.

Up the grand staircase they went, past

murmuring voices and tinkling laughter, gowns, and tuxedos and star-studded diamonds. Everyone that was anyone was there for the opening night.

"And we're here, too," Katie said in rapture.

The lights went down and the audience hushed, every eye on the stage. Slowly, the heavy curtain rose as a hundred voices burst into song. The opera had begun.

Katie watched as Mrs. Hoffman sang from the depths of her heart. And as she watched, she thought back on everything that had happened since that stormy night in Cambria. Suddenly, Katie knew why Aimee Hoffman had come to the tiny sea-side town.

It's just like Beth said, and it's just like Mrs. Hoffman said, and it's just like Leah said . . . Only I was too dumb to admit it.

Mrs. Hoffman had come to escape—escape from her difficult, demanding life. Could it be that a rich, famous person, who seemed to have everything she could possibly desire, sometimes just wanted to be ordinary?

Hmmmm . . . All that glitters is not gold. The little saying went around in Katie's head. Now she knew the answer to the question she had asked under the oak tree!

Perhaps Katie would never be rich or famous, but she already had so much to be thankful for. And if she worked hard, and didn't give up, who knows? One day, her dreams just might come true. Hard work and thankfulness—the perfect formula for success!

Dear Diary,

Well, I'm home again, here in my little town, sitting under my oak tree. I thought I would never want to leave that hotel in New York, but now I'm so happy to be back! I don't think I ever really saw how beautiful it is here — and how peaceful. I could do with some peace and quiet for a while, especially since school starts in two weeks! School, yuck... I'll try not to think about that right now.

After the opera that night, we got to go back stage and meet all the other stars. It was great! I felt so shy, I couldn't even open my mouth to ask anyone any questions. Boy, was I mad at myself afterward.

There were so many things I wanted to find out, but when the time came, I couldn't think of a single word to say! I just walked around with my mouth hanging open. Oh, how embarrassing! At least I wasn't as bad as Beth, though. She was so nervous she tripped over a rope and fell on her face — right in front of Mr. Lorenzo! (He was the BIG man who sang along with Aimee Hoffman.)

Mrs. Hoffman and Leah have promised to come and visit us next summer in Cambria. Mrs. Hoffman loves it here. She says its her favorite place to vacation. Now I think I understand why, though I wasn't able to before.

Maybe I'll have lots of hardships

in my life, just as Aimee Hoffman and Leah have had. I just pray I'll be strong like them, and not give up on my dreams. When I get discouraged, I can think of my two new friends and how they helped me.

I better put my diary back in its little box now. I wouldn't trade it for all the diamonds and rubies in the world, that's for sure! Inside are so many wonderful adventures and discoveries — and there are still lots of pages to be filled!

I guess its time to go meet Beth, so I'll say good-bye. We've got one more baseball game to finish off the season. Tyler Robertson, watch out!